For David

Library of Congress Cataloging in Publication Data

Barklem, Jill.
  Brambly Hedge, summer story.
  SUMMARY: Follows the activities of the Brambly
Hedge community of field mice in summer.
  [1. Mice—Fiction] I. Title.
PZ7.B25058Bt   [E]   80-15423
ISBN 0-399-20747-3   ISBN 0-399-61157-6 (GB)

First published in the United States of America 1980
by Philomel Books
The Putnam Publishing Group,
200 Madison Avenue, New York, N.Y. 10016
Made and printed in Great Britain

SUMMER STORY

Jill Barklem

PHILOMEL BOOKS

It was a very hot summer.

Each day the sun rose high in the blue sky, and the fields shimmered in the heat.

The hedgerow was quiet. Many of the mice preferred to stay inside their shady cottages, trying to keep cool.

Out of doors, the best place to be was down by the stream. The mice gathered there in the afternoon, sat under the bank in the shade, and dangled their paws and tails in the clear water.

On the banks of the stream were the flour and
dairy mills. The flow of the water turned the
wheels which ground the flour and churned
the butter for Brambly Hedge.

Poppy Eyebright looked after the Dairy Stump.
She supervised the large vat into which milk,
kindly given by some friendly cows, was poured
and stored. The many kitchens, where cheeses
were drained and shaped, smoked and wrapped,
were also in her care.

Poppy was not fond of hot weather. Her pats of butter began to melt unless they were wrapped in cool dock leaves, and the pots of cream had to be hung in the millpool to keep them fresh.

When her work was finished she would wander out by the millwheel, enjoying the splashes of cool water.

The flour mill, further down the stream, was run by the miller, Dusty Dogwood. Dogwood was his family name, but he was called Dusty because he was always covered from tail to whiskers with flour dust.

He was a cheerful and friendly mouse,
like his father, his grandfather, and his great-
grandfather, who had all run the mill before him.
He loved the fine weather, and strolled up and
down the stream, chatting to the paddlers and
dabblers.

His walks took him past the Dairy, where
he would often see Poppy standing by the stream,
looking very pretty. As the long, hot days went by,
Dusty used to spend more and more time
walking up to the Dairy, and Poppy used to go
out more and more often to the mossy shadows
of the millwheel . . . .

Early in June, Miss Poppy Eyebright and Mr. Dusty Dogwood officially announced their engagement. Everyone along the hedgerow was delighted.

Midsummer's Day was picked for the wedding, and preparations were started at once. Poppy was so sure the weather would hold that they decided that the wedding should take place on the stream. It was the coolest place, and besides, it was very romantic.

Dusty found a large, flat piece of bark up in the woods, which a party of mice carried down to the water's edge. It was floated, with some difficulty, just under the mill weir, and tethered in midstream by plaited rush and nettle ropes.

Poppy prepared her trousseau. Every afternoon, she sat in the shade of some tall kingcups embroidering her wedding dress, which she hid as soon as she saw anyone coming along the path.

The wedding day dawned at last. The sky
was clear and blue, and it was hotter than ever.
The kitchens of Brambly Hedge were full of
activity. Cool summer foods were being made.
There was cold watercress soup, fresh dandelion
salad, honey creams, syllabubs and meringues.

The young mice had been up early to gather huge baskets of wild strawberries.

Basil selected some white wines, primrose, meadowsweet and elderflower, and hung them to cool in the rushes. Basil was in charge of all the cellars under the Store Stump. He was a stout, good-natured mouse, with long white whiskers, and a sensitive nose for fine wine.

In her rooms above the Dairy, Poppy dressed carefully. She polished her whiskers, and dabbed rosewater behind her ears. Her straw bonnet, which Lady Woodmouse had trimmed with flowers, hung from the bedpost, and her bridal posy lay waiting on the windowsill. She peeped at her reflection in the shiny wardrobe door, took a deep breath, and ran downstairs to join her bridesmaids.

Dusty kept his best suit in a basket under the stairs to protect it from the moths. He put it on, and tucked a daisy in his buttonhole.

"I'd better just check that barley I ground yesterday," he said to himself. He ran up the steps at such a pace that the whole mill seemed to shake. The wooden floor above him let down a cloud of dust, all over his new wedding suit.

"Bother it!" he said, sitting on a sack of corn, and looking at his mottled jacket in dismay.

There was a thumping on the door below, and his friend Conker called through the letterbox,

"Dusty, are you ready? It's nearly time to go."

Dusty sighed, and went morosely down the stairs.

As soon as Conker saw him, he began to giggle. "Dusty by name, dusty by nature," he said, trying to remedy matters with his clean handkerchief.

The floury dust swirled, and settled again on whiskers, tails, best clothes and buttonholes. The two mice looked at each other, and started to laugh. They laughed so much that they had to sit down on a flour bag to recover.

The wedding was to take place at midday, and Dusty and Conker arrived just in time. The guests were all in their finest clothes. Three young mice, dressed in smart blue suits, had been chosen as pages, and were busily directing everyone to their places. Mrs. Apple discreetly tried to dust down the groom and best man, but to little avail.

At last old Mrs. Eyebright, Poppy's grandmother, spotted the bride and her little bridesmaids coming through the grass. The pages squeaked with excitement, and got into place. Every head turned to watch the bride as she made her way through the buttercups and stepped onto the decorated raft.

The Old Vole, who had been asked to perform the ceremony, stood up, and said in a kindly voice: "Poppy Eyebright, do you love Dusty Dogwood, and will you love him and care for him

for ever and ever?'' Poppy vowed that she would.
  "Dusty Dogwood, do you love Poppy, and will
you love her and look after her for ever and ever?''
  "I will,'' said Dusty. Mrs. Apple blew her nose.

"Then in the name of the flowers and the fields, the stars in the sky, and the streams that flow down to the sea, and the mystery that breathes wonder into all these things, I pronounce you mouse and wife."

All the mice cheered as Dusty kissed his bride, and the bridesmaids threw baskets of petals over the happy couple. Mrs. Apple wiped a tear from her eye, and the dancing and feasting began.

First they danced, for no one could keep still, jigs, reels and quadrilles.

Mr. Apple proposed a toast.

"To the bride and groom! May their tails grow long, and their eyes be bright, and all their squeaks be little ones."

The guests raised their glasses, and then they danced again. The dancing was so vigorous that the raft bobbed up and down. Gradually the ropes holding the raft began to wear through.

One by one, the little ropes snapped, until finally the very last one gave way.

They were carried into midstream by the current. The young mice squeaked with alarm at first, but as they seemed to come to no harm, they continued with the feast.

The raft floated gently past fields of buttercups and meadowsweet, and the voles tending the fires in the Pottery came out to wave as the wedding party drifted by.

Eventually, the raft was caught in a leafy clump of rushes and forget-me-nots. The ropes were made fast, and the dancing began again.

At last the dusk came, golden and misty over the
fields. The blue sky slowly darkened, and the mice
began to think about getting home. All the food
was finished up, and the pots and pans hidden in
the rushes to be collected the next day.

They walked back through the fields in the evening sun, looking very splendid in their wedding clothes. The Old Vole was taken back to his hole first, and the rest of the mice gradually made their way home to bed, exhausted but happy.

And what happened to Poppy and Dusty?
They slipped quietly away to the primrose
woods. The primroses were over, but there,
hidden amongst the long grass and ferns, wild
roses and honeysuckle, was the cottage in which
they had chosen to stay.

It was the perfect place for a honeymoon.